DAMIAN DROOTH, SUPERSLEUTH

How to be a Detective

KT-145-225

Other TIGERS by Barbara Mitchelhill

DAMIAN DROOTH, SUPERSLEUTH

How to be a Detective

Barbara Mitchelhill
Illustrated by Tony Ross

Andersen Press • London

For Louise, Lucy, Max, Tom and Felix –
also for Isabel (who especially like notes
on Criminal Types)

First published in 2004 by
Andersen Press Limited,
20 Vauxhall Bridge Road, London SW1V 2SA
www.andersenpress.co.uk

British Library Cataloguing in Publication Data
available
ISBN 1 84270 360 9

Phototypeset by Intype Libra Ltd
Printed and bound in Great Britain by
Bookmarque Ltd, Croydon, Surrey

Chapter 1

My name is Damian Drooth and I'm a mega successful detective. You might have heard of me. I've solved loads of crimes in our town.

Not long ago, I decided that there must be masses of kids who wanted to learn to be crime busters like me. So I put a sign in the school playground that read:

DAMIAN DROOTH, FAMUS
DETECTIVE AND SURPERSLOOTH
WILL GIVE A TALK ON HOW TO
SPOT CROOKS AND THEEVES AND
CRIMINLES ON THE STREETS.
COME TO THE SHED AT THE
BOTOME OF THE GARDEN AT 10
O'CLOCK ON SATERDAY MORNIGN.
WARE SHADES.
DO NOT BE LAIT.

Entruns fee: 1 pakit of crisps.

I chose Saturday because Mum was working that day. She has a business called Home Cooking Unlimited. She makes cakes and sandwiches and takes them to weddings and things. She likes to keep busy. I think she gets bored just hanging around the house.

Sometimes I go along and help her – but I didn't want to go this time. She was doing the food at a flower show. (I'm not keen on flowers.)

'I'll stay and do my homework,' I said. 'I've got this really interesting essay to do for history.'

I noticed Mum tightened her lips and screwed up her eyes. I call this her Suspicious Look.

'That doesn't sound like you, Damian,' she said. 'What are you up to?'

I didn't say anything. I just stood there looking hurt. But it did the trick.

In the end, she said, 'All right, then. But you have to stay in the house. I'll ask Mrs Robertson next door to pop round and keep an eye on you.'

Of course I agreed. If I hadn't, I would have spent Saturday at the flower show washing up and listening to people talk about fertilisers and greenfly.

Chapter 2

On Saturday morning, Mum was late loading the van. I'd almost finished my breakfast and she was still flashing in and out of the kitchen. In a rush as usual.

'Carry something out for me, will you, Damian?' she panted (showing how unfit she is).

'OK,' I said. I put down my toast and picked up a chocolate gateau. My favourite.

'No, not that,' said Mum and
grabbed it off me. 'Carry the cutlery.'
So I did. But even this didn't please
her. I know I dropped the box but
nothing was broken and I picked up
every last knife and fork. Except the
ones that fell down the drain.

In the end, she drove off at nine
o'clock which was great timing

because the kids arrived soon after for the Detective School. They formed a long line outside the garden shed. It was obvious they were dead keen to learn.

Tod Browning and his sister, Lavender, were at the front of the queue. So they got the seats. 'The early detective catches the worm,' I always say (or something like that).

I collected the entrance fees (7 bags of crisps in all) which I stashed away in a box before standing on a bucket ready to give my first talk.

'Right,' I said. 'I want to check that you've got your notebooks and pencils. Every good detective should have one.' They had.

Now I needed to impress them. I didn't say a thing. I just got out my press cuttings from the local paper.

DAMIAN DROOTH SAVES DIRECTOR'S DAUGHTER

Police were astonished when a young boy, Damian Drooth, saved the young daughter of a film director kidnapped by an international crook.

DAMIAN DROOTH FINDS STOLEN DIAMONDS

A diamond necklace belonging to a pop star was recovered by a local boy detective. Damian Drooth was guarding presents worth thousands of pounds at the wedding of Pop Star, Tiger Lily, to footballer, Gary Blaze.

I could see they were gobsmacked. Then they started asking questions.

'Don't the police get mad because you're cleverer than they are?'

'Did any crooks pay you big money to stop you telling on them?'

That kind of thing.

Lavender Browning, who was only a small kid, asked me, 'Whath's it like to be famouth, Damian?'

'Yeah, go on. Tell us,' the rest shouted.

But I was too modest to answer. Instead, I began to explain my Theories of Criminal Detection. After all, they were here to learn.

'These are the most common types of crooks you're likely to spot,' I said and I pinned two posters (drawn by me) on the wall.

CRIMINLE TIPE NO. 1
EYES SET CLOSE TOGETHER
(A good egrample is Mr Forrester in
Class 5.
Wotch owt for him in fewcher.)

CRIMINLE TIPE NO. 2
ENYBODY WITH A BEERD
(yooshully men)
BLACK BEERDS ARE THE WURST.
(Take a look at the new crossing
atendent.
He cud be up to no gud. Only tiem
will tell.)

Some of them were scribbling like
mad in their notebooks. Some of them
were yawning with the exhaustion of
listening and learning. I feel just like
that in Mr Johnson's maths class.

'Always remember,' I said, 'the best
way to learn how to track down
criminals is to be alert.'

15

'How do we do that, Damian?' Harry Houseman called out.

I explained. 'If we went down to the High Street and stayed alert, we'd probably spot a criminal.'

'In our High Street?'

'Absolutely,' I said.

'Then let's do it!' said Tod.

I shook my head. 'Not today.'

The fact was, I was secretly looking forward to eating the crisps before Mum came back. Anyway, I'd promised to stay in and I always keep my promises. Almost always.

'Come on, Damian,' shouted Winston Hunt. 'What are you scared of?'

'Yeah!' called out one of the girls. 'Show us how it's done – if you can.'

Then everybody joined in. There was nearly a riot. They were so keen. How could I refuse? So we set off.

Chapter 3

'Just remember what I told you,' I said
when we'd reached the High Street.
'Look out for the most common types
of crooks. Check your notes, if you
need to.'

We were just passing Woolworth's
when Lavender tugged at my sleeve.

'Over there, Damian. Look! A
cwiminal!'

A man with a beard was riding one
of those buggy things along the
pavement. His beard was white, so he
wasn't a major criminal. But I didn't
like to point this out.

'Mmm,' I said. 'Maybe he is . . . Or maybe not.'

But Lavender, who got easily excited, was absolutely convinced. 'He'th a wobber. He'th going to mug thomebody and take their money. I can tell.'

'OK. OK,' I said. 'I'll show you how to keep a close watch on him. Follow me.'

I pressed my back up against the wall, my cap pulled down over my eyes. All the other kids did the same. We kept our eyes fixed on the suspect as he came down the High Street. Then – just as Lavender had thought – he started heading towards a woman who was collecting for charity. And the tin was **full of money!**

'He'th going to thteal it,' said Lavender. 'What can we do?'

Harry Houseman, the biggest boy in our class, couldn't wait to be in on the action. 'Right, Lavender! I'll stop him!'

He darted forward between the buggy and the collector. He stopped, held his hand in the air and shouted, 'Don't come any closer!'

The man in the buggy-thing looked shocked. He tried to swerve to avoid Harry – or maybe he was making a getaway. I don't know which. Whatever his plans were, they were foiled. The

buggy-thing tipped over and the man went sprawling on the pavement. So he never got his hands on the collecting tin. Seconds later, there were loads of people round him. He had no chance of getting away.

Another job well done.

'Come on,' I called to Harry. 'Never stay on the scene of the crime once you've solved it.'

Chapter 4

Things were going well and I had a brilliant idea.

'I want to try out a new theory,' I said. 'You can all come with me if you like.'

'Oh yeth, Damian,' said Lavender. 'Where are we going?'

'The library,' I said. 'We can do some people-watching without anybody noticing us.'

The theory I was working on was this: people with thin lips were inclined to be crooks. Stealing jewels. Breaking into banks. That kind of thing. I worked this out from looking at the photos in the local paper. Going into the library would give me the chance to see if my theory was true.

So we walked in, took some books off the shelves and sat at the tables. Of course, everybody thought we were reading – but we weren't. We were peering over the top of the books, looking for criminal types.

We watched for at least ten minutes and then Lavender hissed, 'Pssst!' She was trying to attract my attention.

She was nodding in the direction of the librarian's desk where a large woman with a fur coat and frothy blonde hair was taking out a book. 'I think thee's one,' she whispered.

I got up and sidled over to the desk, hoping no one would notice. The other kids followed. When I got near, I could see that the woman was borrowing a suspicious book called *Loot*. (A technical term for stolen goods known only to experienced detectives.)

This was not the only suspicious thing. The woman's eyes were close together, cunningly hidden by glasses. **But best of all** – her lips were thin and tight and there were little wrinkles

round them. Bingo! She was an
excellent example of all my Criminal
Types (except she didn't have a
beard).

I turned to Lavender and gave her a thumbs-up. The kid might make a brilliant detective – one day.

Unfortunately, we were getting funny looks from Miss Travis, the librarian. I don't know why. She is usually very understanding. She must have had a headache or something.

The blonde woman put the book in her bag, ready to go. As she turned and headed for the door, I gave a signal for the others to follow. But at this point, my luck changed.

'Damian!' Miss Travis called. 'Please will you and your friends put away those books before you leave?'

I gritted my teeth and gave her one of my best smiles.

'We'll do it later,' I said. 'We've just got to . . .'

'NOW!' she shouted. Miss Travis never shouts. She was clearly not feeling well.

We rushed over to the table, stuck the books back on the shelves and

26

dashed out of the library. The High
Street was crowded with shoppers.
Had I lost the thin-lipped woman
forever? I wondered.

'She's there!' said Harry, who was so
tall he could see over people's heads.
'She's level with that white van.'

Luckily she stood out from the crowd (what with her big blonde hair and her fur coat and that). We all raced after her down the High Street, which was not easy as people kept crashing into us.

'Keep your eyes fixed on her,' I panted. 'We need to know what she's up to.'

But before we could catch her, she turned into the Building Society.

'We've got to stop her,' I said. 'She's probably doing a raid.'

It was the very worst of luck that, at that moment, I bumped into Mr Robertson from next door.

'Hey, hey, hey, young Damian,' he said, grabbing hold of my shoulders. 'What are you doing in town? Your mother said you were staying at home.'

I didn't know what to say.

'You'd better come with me,' he said. 'My wife will be worried silly, wondering where you are.'

I looked round at the would-be detectives.

'Sorry, guys. Something's turned up. I've got to go.'

Now we'd never find out about the blonde with the thin lips.

Chapter 5

When Mum came home, I could tell she'd had a tough day. She looked really stressed.

'I've had two calls on my mobile,' she said. 'One from Sue Greenspan who was collecting for charity outside Woolworth's. And one from Elizabeth Travis at the library.'

She glared at me. 'Why were you running riot through the town this morning with a gang of hooligans? Knocking down old people. Wrecking the library. Can't I trust you for half a day, Damian?'

I hate it when she shouts. I try to understand. But it's hard on a kid who only needs a kind word and a plate of chips.

'Tomorrow,' she said, 'you're coming with me – like it or not. I'm catering at the local dog show and I'm not leaving you behind to get into more trouble. You can watch the dogs.'

Actually, I like dogs. So the dog show was cool.

I made quick phone calls to the kids who had come to the Detective School that morning.

'Be at the County Exhibition Hall by ten o'clock tomorrow for another training session,' I said. 'Bring a dog if you've got one.' (This was good thinking. No one would suspect kids with dogs were working as undercover trainee detectives.)

By the time I arrived with Mum, the dog show was in full swing.

I offered to help carry the food from the van. Mum's not all that fit at her age. But no. She wouldn't let me.

'I'll manage by myself, thank you, Damian,' she said. 'It's safer.'

So I left her to it and went and
settled into a ringside seat. Tod and
Lavender had already arrived with
their dog, Curly. Winston walked in
soon after with Thumper who smelled
really bad.

'Harry's coming later,' he said, 'but I
don't think the rest are keen to go
sleuthing on a Sunday.'

'Their loss,' I said. 'They'll never make the grade without the practice.'

At this point, Lavender started tugging at my sleeve in an agitated sort of way.

'Damian!' she said. 'I've theen her.'

'Seen who?'

'That blonde woman with the thin lipth. The one planning to wob the building thothiety.'

I took out my shades and put them on. At once, I was alert and ready for action. I looked round the hall, my eyes peeled.

'Over there!' said Lavender, waggling her finger. 'Thee's right in the middle of the ring! Look! Thee's the JUDGE!'

I could hardly believe it. The blonde was there all right and wearing a huge rosette. Here was my biggest chance yet to catch a crook red-handed. Not to mention the chance to prove my Criminal Theory number 3.

This is the plan I wrote.

Lavinder, Winston and Harry to do:
stay neer the show ring
wotch owt for Mum if she comes
looking for me.

Me to do:
follow suspeckt when she leeves ring
take notes on criminle aktivitees
contact Inspeckter Crockitt
tawk to the press and TV

Inspeckter Crockitt to do:
Arrest suspeckt
Put suspeckt in jale

We all sat and watched while the blonde woman judged the Small Dog competition. First she looked at one dog. Then the next. It took ages to check them all. I don't know why. It was obvious which was the best dog.

When she finally announced the winner, I was quite disgusted. The dog had hair right down to its feet and a stupid red bow on its head. It was owned by someone called Major Dalrymple. How would he like it if someone tied a bow in his hair (if he had any)?

She gave him a silver cup and a certificate and then she walked out of the ring.

'Right,' I said. 'I'm going to follow her. See what information I can get.'

I needed more hard facts if I was going to call the police and have her arrested.

'Take Curly with you,' said Lavender. 'Thee's a good guard dog. Dangerwoush teeth!'

I shrugged. I didn't need protection. I'm used to danger.

But Lavender insisted. 'You might get into a weally twicky thituation.'

Just to please Lavender, I did.

Outside the hall, I spotted the judge heading towards the refreshment room. The only snag was, Mum was in there, too.

I kept my wits sharp. I needed a disguise. There was a small changing room nearby and I found a large hat and a coat that fitted me, sort of. Not even my own mother would recognise me now.

I went into the refreshment room, tied Curly to the table leg and began to observe the blonde.

Aktivitees of criminle blond wuman.
Puts 3 teespoons of shuger in tee.
Drinks tee.
Openz bag
Takes role of banknotes owt of bag
and cownts them!!!!!!!!!!!!!!!
Duz this meen she did raid on
Bilding Sossiety?
Probably!!!!!!!!!!!!!!!

Just as I'd finished writing my notes, I saw Mum come out of the kitchen. She was carrying one of her chocolate gateaux. (My favourite.) It was too much for me. Even the best detectives need a break sometimes.

I decided that if I went up to the counter with my head well down, I could buy a slice and she'd never notice. But I forgot about Curly. She decided to follow me, dragging the table with her and wrapping her lead round a waiter's legs.

'Oy, you!' he said (very rudely, I thought). 'You can't bring dogs in here. You'll have to take him out.'

'It's a "her" actually,' I said.

At the sound of my voice, Mum looked up. 'Damian?' she said. 'What are you doing here? I told you to go and watch the show.'

'Sorry, Mum,' I said. 'I felt faint. I thought a piece of your gateau would make me feel better.'

She could have looked a bit more sympathetic but anyway, she cut a massive slice and put it on a paper plate.

'Go back to the show ring,' she said, 'and take that heap of hair with you.' (A mean way to describe Curly.)

'Righto, Mum,' I said and began to walk away with the gateau in one hand and Curly's lead in the other.

'And for goodness sake take off that ridiculous coat!' she called after me. She didn't realise I was in disguise. It's tough working undercover.

During all the fuss with Mum and the waiter, I had taken my eyes off the blonde. Big mistake. When I glanced over to her table, she was gone. Maybe she suspected that I was watching her. Maybe she'd made a run for it. Whatever – I wasn't going to let her get away.

Chapter 6

When I got back to the show ring Lavender amazed me once again with her powers of detection.

She looked at me and said, 'I thee you've been eating chocolate cake, Damian.'

How did she guess? The kid's a genius!

Unfortunately, I had to tell her that our suspect had given me the slip. 'Once they know you're on to them,' I said, 'things can get really tough.'

Lavender looked puzzled. 'But ithn't that her?' she said, pointing to the far side of the ring, behind the last row of seats. The suspect was standing there talking to someone.

'You've got laser eyes, you have,' said Harry.'

'Yeah!' said Winston. 'Well spotted, Lavender.'

'Brilliant,' said Tod.

No good getting too excited. There was real detective work still to be done – and I was going to do it.

'Right,' I said. 'I'm going to sneak over there.'

'But thee might thee you, Damian!' said Lavender.

'Cool it, Lavender. Nobody will see me. I can be almost invisible when I need to be. Watch and learn.'

Perfecting this skill had taken a lot of practice – in the kitchen, down the corridors at school, in the cinema. I had studied for months. Now was my chance to put it to use in preventing crime.

I dropped down flat onto the floor. Slowly, I moved forward keeping my body in contact with the ground, Commando fashion. It was not an easy exercise.

This took time but when I got round to the other side, the blonde was still there, talking to a man who looked familiar. Lucky or what? To get as close as possible, I hid under a seat in

the back row. Then I pressed my ear to the ground and listened.

'... wasn't enough money ...'

'The risk is too great ...'

'... greedy ...'

'... plan carefully ...'

I couldn't hear every word for a very good reason – Curly had followed me and was stuffing her nose in my face. I tried pushing her away but she started whining and almost gave the game away.

I might not have heard everything the blonde said but I heard enough. It was obvious that she was discussing the Building Society. I set off to go back with Curly in tow, to tell the others.

'They're planning a robbery,' I said as I sat down. 'And that man she's talking to – I've seen him before. I think he works at the Building Society.'

'Typical,' said Winston. 'He's in on it.'

I nodded wisely.

'Tho he'th a cwook, too!' said Lavender. 'You've got to do something to thtop them, Damian.'

She trusted me. I had to act fast.

'Lend me your mobile, Lavender,' I said. 'I'm going to ring Inspector Crockitt.'

Chapter 7

I left a message for the Inspector. It was perfectly clear.

'Come quick and arrest the judge at the Dog Show who is a dangerous bank robber.'

But the police can be very slow. A whole hour passed – and no one came.

Maybe the desk sergeant I spoke to hadn't written it down properly. Maybe he hadn't passed it on to Inspector Crockitt.

'Funny,' I said to the others. 'I thought he'd be here like a shot.'

'I don't think the police are coming,' said Harry. 'We're running out of time. The competition's nearly finished.'

Harry was right. The Large Dog competition was the last in the show. Our suspect was about to award the cup to the winner. Soon, I'd have to go home with Mum and another criminal would have escaped.

Suddenly, Winston stood up in his seat and pointed. 'Hey! Look who's got the cup,' he said. 'It's that major who won the other competition.'

Winston had obviously learned my lessons about staying alert.

'That's not a major,' I said, staring into the ring. 'He's the judge's partner in crime. They're planning a robbery. I heard them talking.'

'Cor!' said Winston. 'Then we've got to act now. We can't wait for the police.'

'What thall we do, Damian?' Lavender asked.

I thought about it. Then I gave the kids instructions – just simple things to do. I would cope with the dangerous stuff myself.

This is what happened.

I ran into the centre of the show ring. Hundreds of pairs of eyes were on me but I didn't care.

The judge (our suspect) looked horrified.

'Clear off!' she shouted. 'You're ruining the contest.'

But I refused to move. Instead, I turned to the people in the middle of the show ring standing with their dogs.

'This judge is a criminal,' I said. 'She's not fit to hand out cups. She's a thief.'

At that moment, the blonde bolted for the exit – and so did the major. It was just what I expected. But I was ready for them. I gave the signal to my trainee detectives and they released their dogs shouting, 'Go, go, go!' Then Curly and Thumper chased after the two crooks.

'Aaaahhhhgggg!' screamed the blonde and tripped over a loose piece of carpet.'

'Noooooo!' yelled the major and tripped over the blonde.

'Woof, woof, woof!' barked the dogs and landed on top of them both.

The dogs in the competition joined in. Barking and yelping and jumping about. It was brilliant!

Security guards came shouting, 'Get those dogs off. They're dangerous!'

I stood there watching. Another
crime solved. Another crook punished.
But it didn't turn out exactly as I'd
planned. I suddenly found myself in
the grip of a burly security guard. I
was furious.

'What are you doing?' I demanded.
'Don't you know who I am?'

'You're the one that's caused this
riot,' he said.

I was shocked. 'But it's her you should be arresting,' I said, pointing to a leg sticking out from the pile of excited dogs.

The security guards didn't seem to know what to do. By the time Inspector Crockitt arrived, our chief suspect and the major were still stuck and calling for help. It was only when four police officers managed to pull the dogs off, that the criminals emerged, shaking and terrified.

'I confess. I confess,' said the judge.

Now this was what I wanted to hear.

The next day, there were big headlines in the local paper.

DAMIAN DOES IT AGAIN. DOG SHOW JUDGE HEADS FOR JAIL.

All the kids at school gathered round to read it.

'You're a bwilliant detective,' said Lavender.

'Yeah,' said Winston. 'Catching a bank robber like that.'

It was good to feel appreciated. But then Harry decided to read the article from start to finish. Every word.

'Wait a minute,' he said as he reached the bottom. 'It doesn't mention a bank robbery here. Or a building society, for that matter.'

I shrugged. 'So?'

'It says that the judge was being paid by the major for letting his dogs win.' He smirked and put down the paper. 'You were just lucky, Damian.'

Did it matter? I had solved a crime, hadn't I?

'If you athk me,' said Lavender, 'cheating at competitions is jutht as bad as wobbing banks. Don't you know that the major could thell puppieth for loths and loths of money if the pawents were pwize winners?'

Of course, I knew that. But I didn't say anything. I just nodded.

The following week, Inspector Crockitt called at school to talk about my part in solving the crime. He went on about not doing dangerous things and finding an adult when we're in trouble. All basic stuff really. I'd heard it loads of times.

Before he left, the Inspector wanted
to have a quiet word with me. (He
likes to pick up tips on how to solve
crimes.) But today I could only
suggest he speeded up his response
time.

'You got to the dog show ages after I
left the message for you,' I said.

'Sorry, Damian,' he replied. 'I
thought it was a joke.'

'A joke?'

'Yes, I wasn't sure the message was from you.'

I nearly choked. Is this the way to run a police force?

I have now thought of how to avoid mistakes like this in future. I have written to Inspector Crockitt outlining my idea for a secret code. It will be known only to the two of us. I can send messages as often as I like with tip-offs about suspected criminals. It's a brilliant idea and I think he'll be dead pleased.

I'm just waiting for a reply.